FESTIVAL READERS

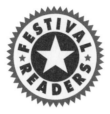

UNIVERSAL PICTURES PRESENTS IN ASSOCIATION WITH MARVEL ENTERPRISES A VALHALLA MOTION PICTURES / GOOD MACHINE PRODUCTION AN ANG LEE FILM "THE HULK"
ERIC BANA JENNIFER CONNELLY SAM ELLIOTT JOSH LUCAS AND NICK NOLTE MUSIC BY MYCHAEL DANNA COSTUME DESIGNER MARIT ALLEN EDITOR TIM SQUYRES ACE PRODUCTION DESIGNER RICK HEINRICHS
DIRECTOR OF PHOTOGRAPHY FREDERICK ELMES ASC EXECUTIVE PRODUCERS STAN LEE KEVIN FEIGE PRODUCED BY GALE ANNE HURD AVI ARAD JAMES SCHAMUS LARRY FRANCO WRITTEN BY JAMES SCHAMUS DIRECTED BY ANG LEE

MARVEL THIS FILM IS NOT YET RATED SPECIAL VISUAL EFFECTS AND ANIMATION BY INDUSTRIAL LIGHT & MAGIC www.thehulk.com A UNIVERSAL PICTURE UNIVERSAL



The Hulk™: *The Hulk Escapes*

Printed in the U.S.A.
Library of Congress catalog card number: 2002114407.
www.harperchildrens.com

1 2 3 4 5 6 7 8 9 10

First Edition

# HULK™

## THE HULK ESCAPES

Adaptation by Acton Figueroa
Based on the Motion Picture Screenplay
Written by James Schamus
Illustrations by Shawn McKelvey

**HarperFestival®**
*A Division of* HarperCollins*Publishers*

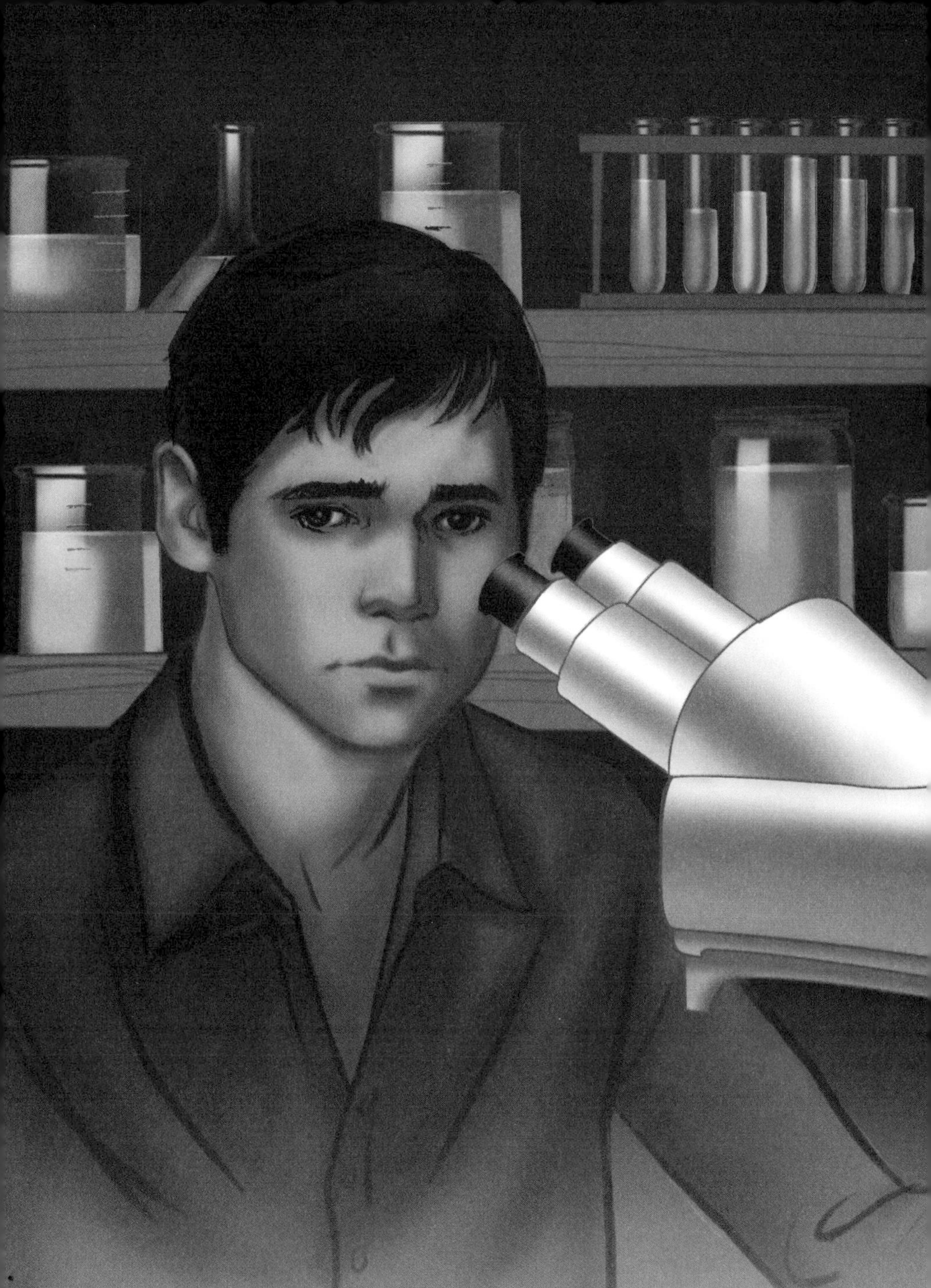

It's not easy being Bruce Banner.

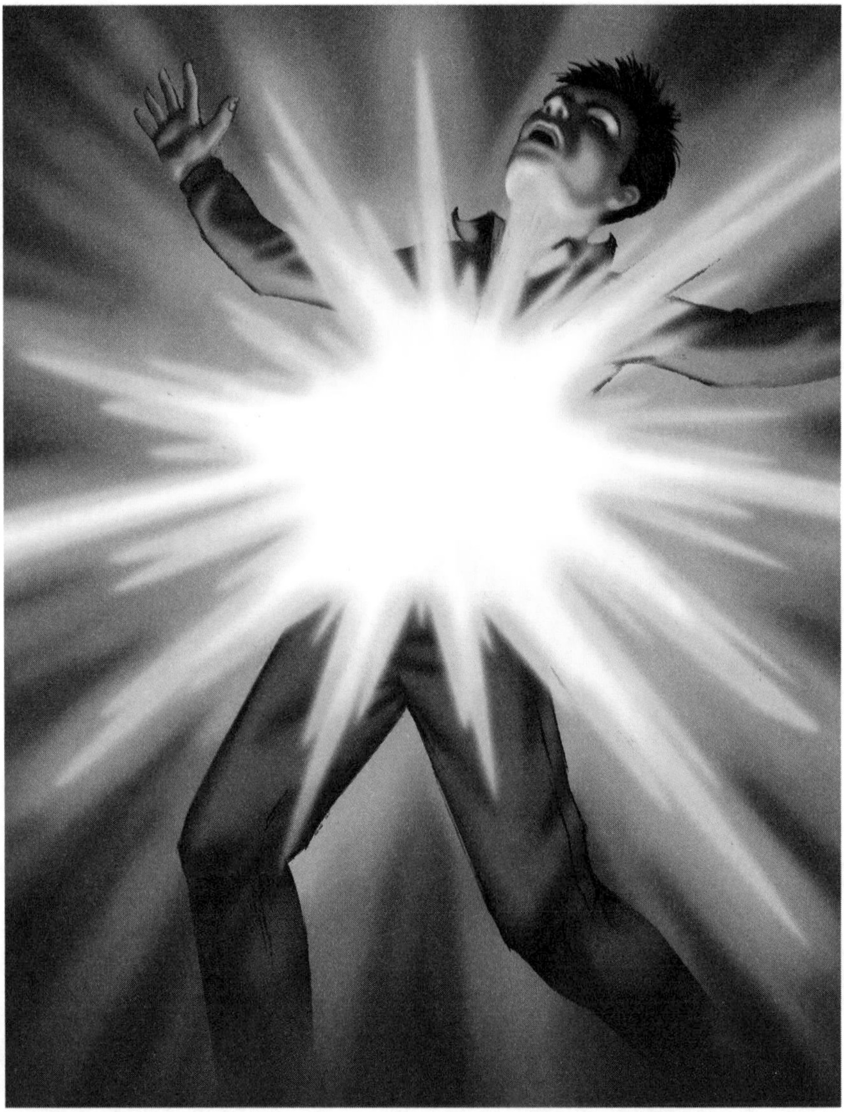

He was just an ordinary scientist
until he had an accident in his lab.
Now, whenever he gets mad, he changes.

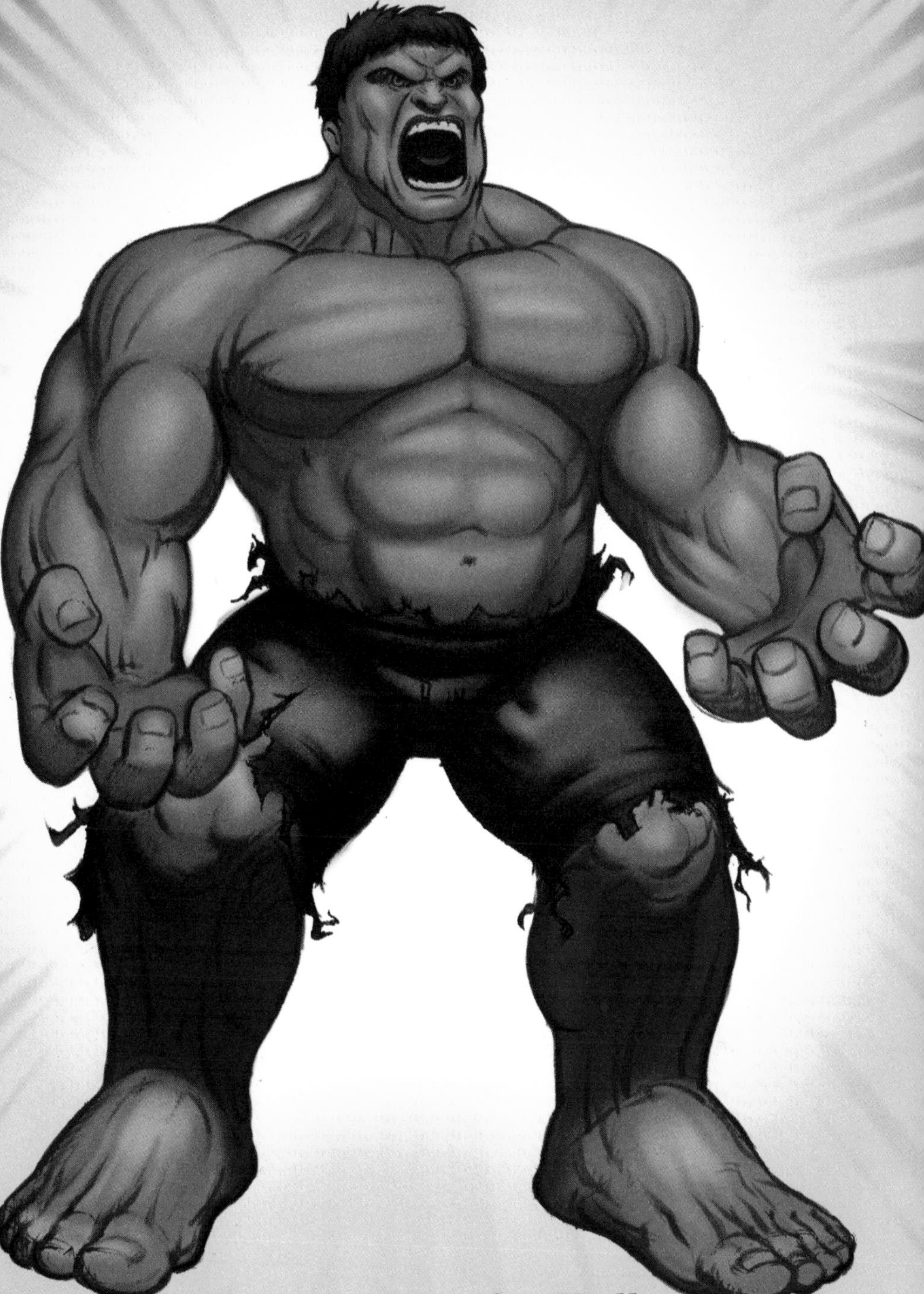

He turns into the Hulk.

Bruce is not an ordinary scientist anymore.

Now other scientists want to study him.

They want to find out what makes him

change into the Hulk.

But the scientists are scared of Bruce.

So he is locked inside this metal cell.

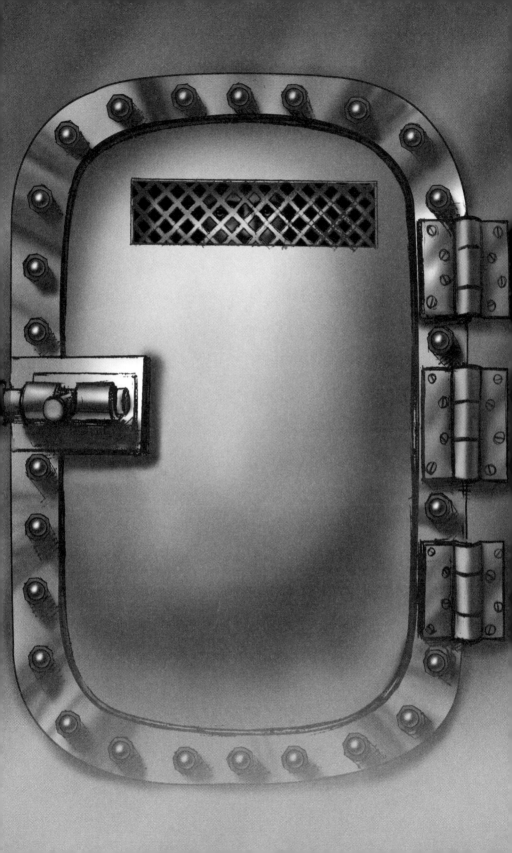

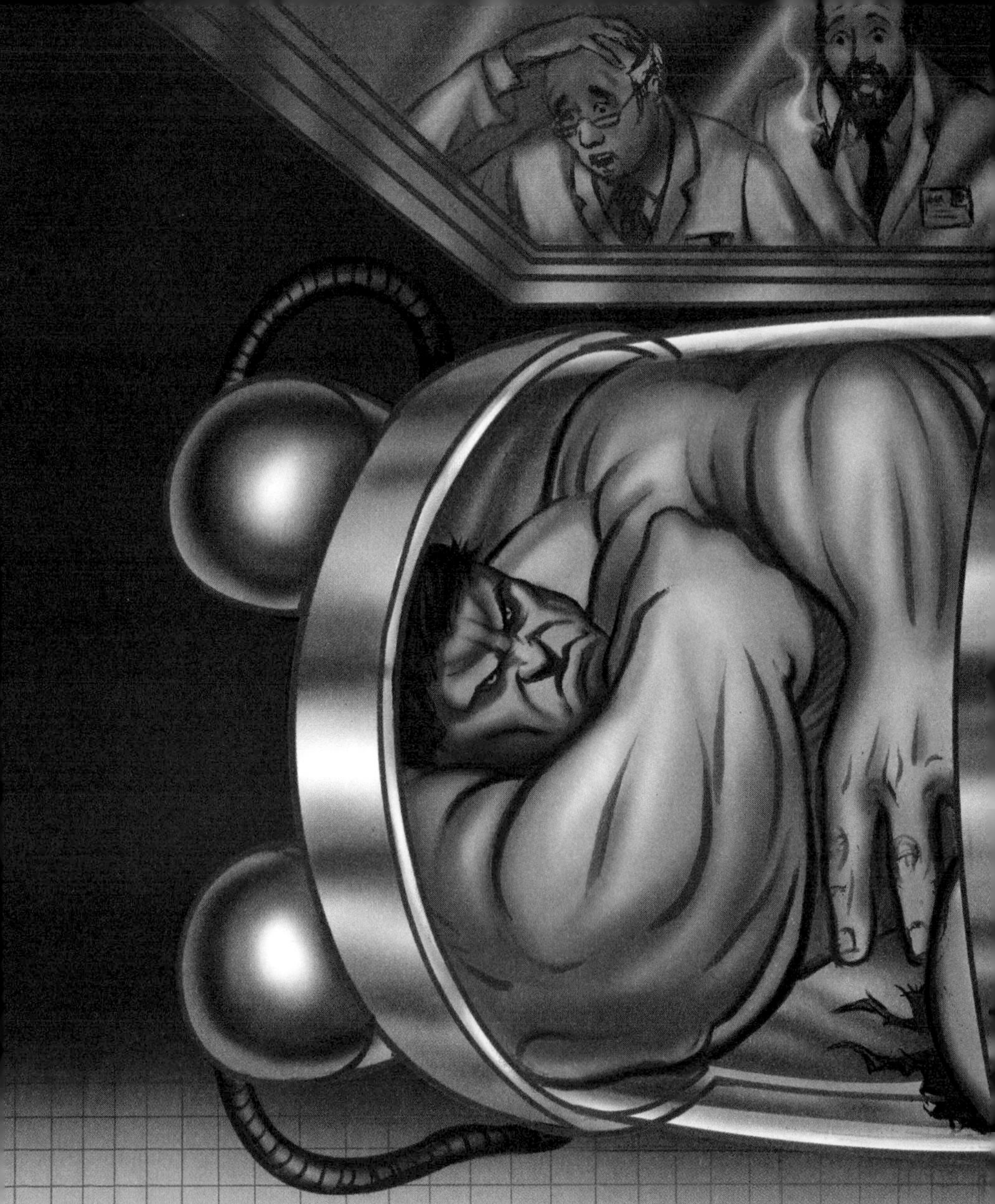

Bruce doesn't like being poked
and prodded by doctors.
It makes him mad.

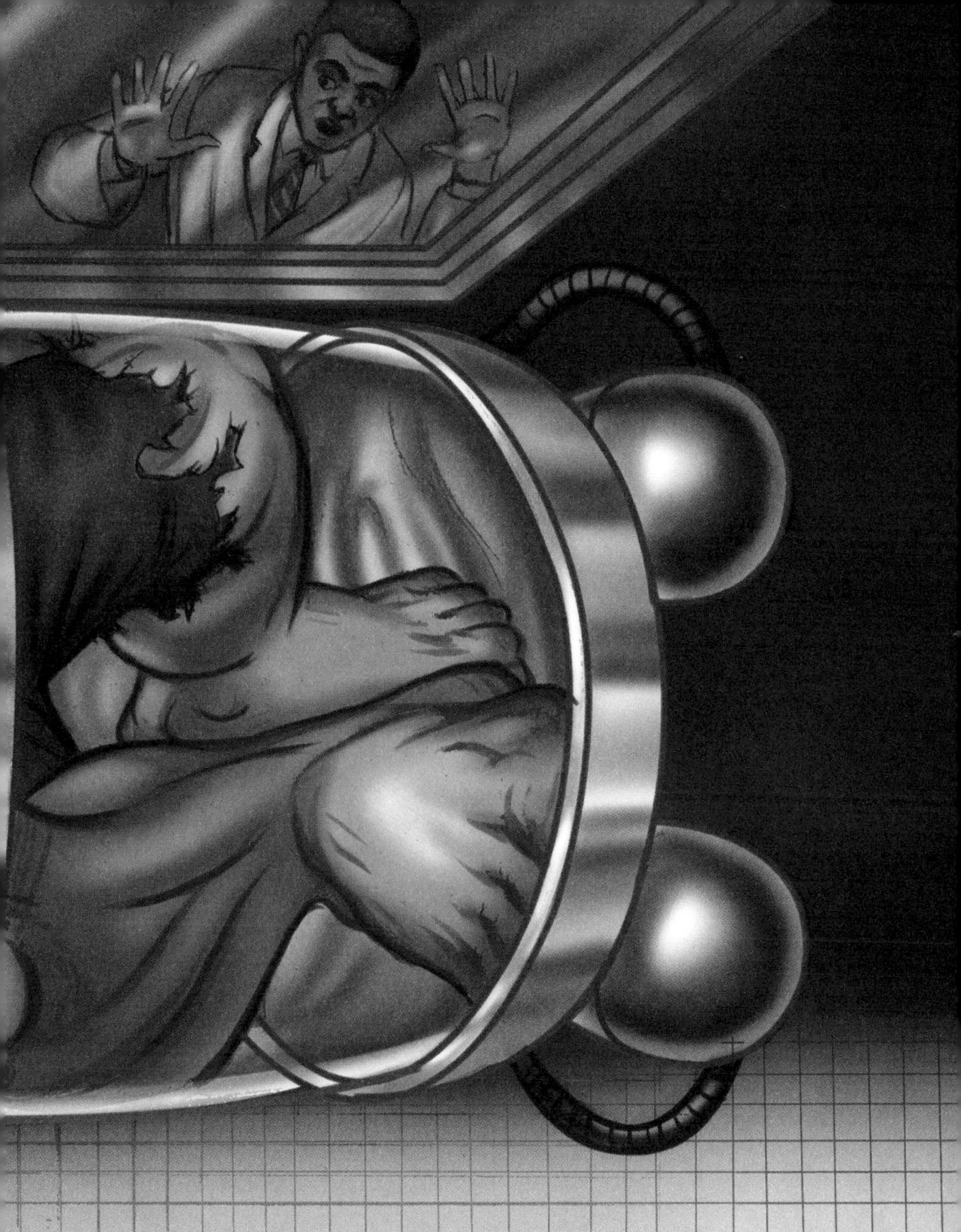

When Bruce gets mad . . .

. . . watch out!

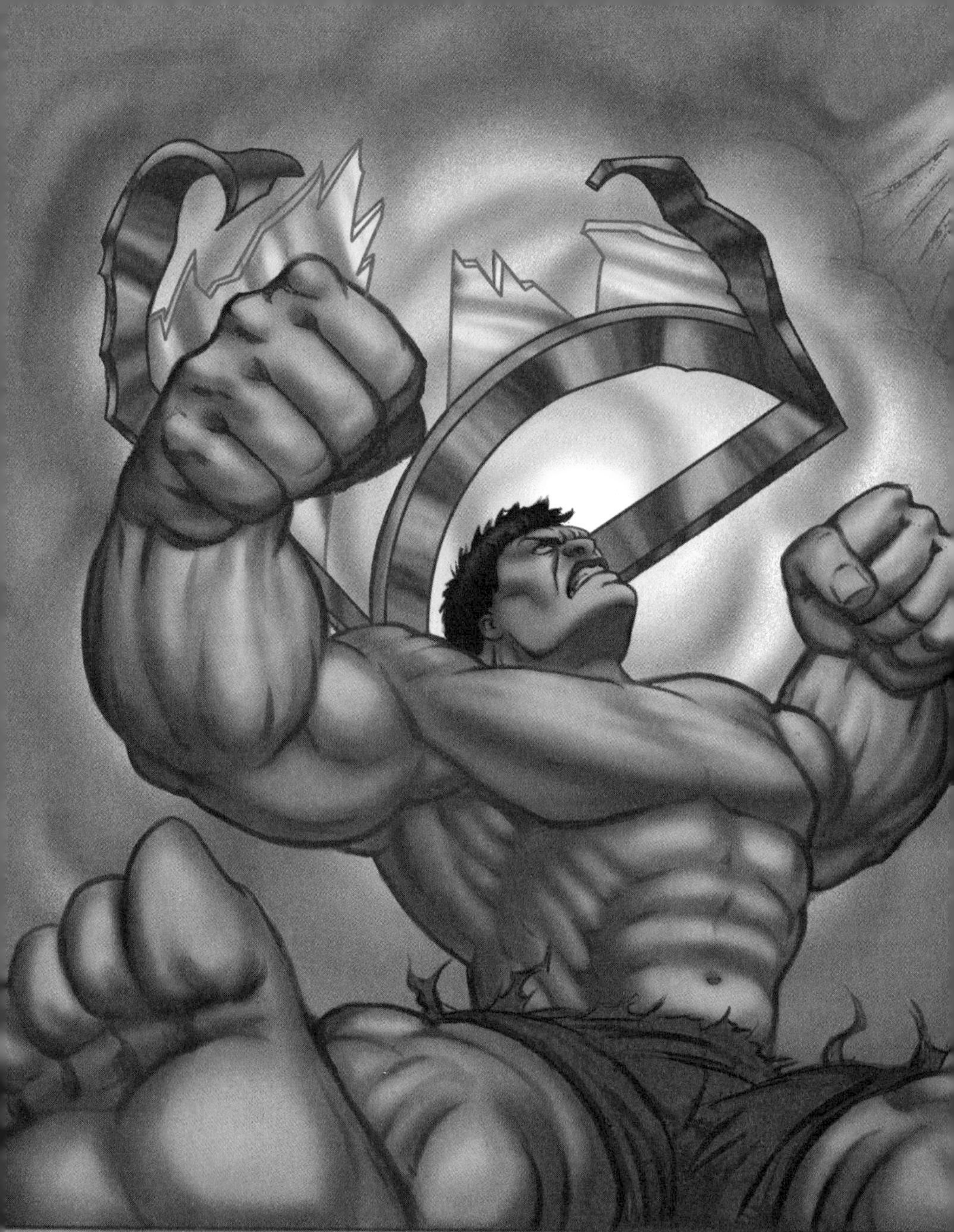

The scientists want to control the Hulk.

But can they?

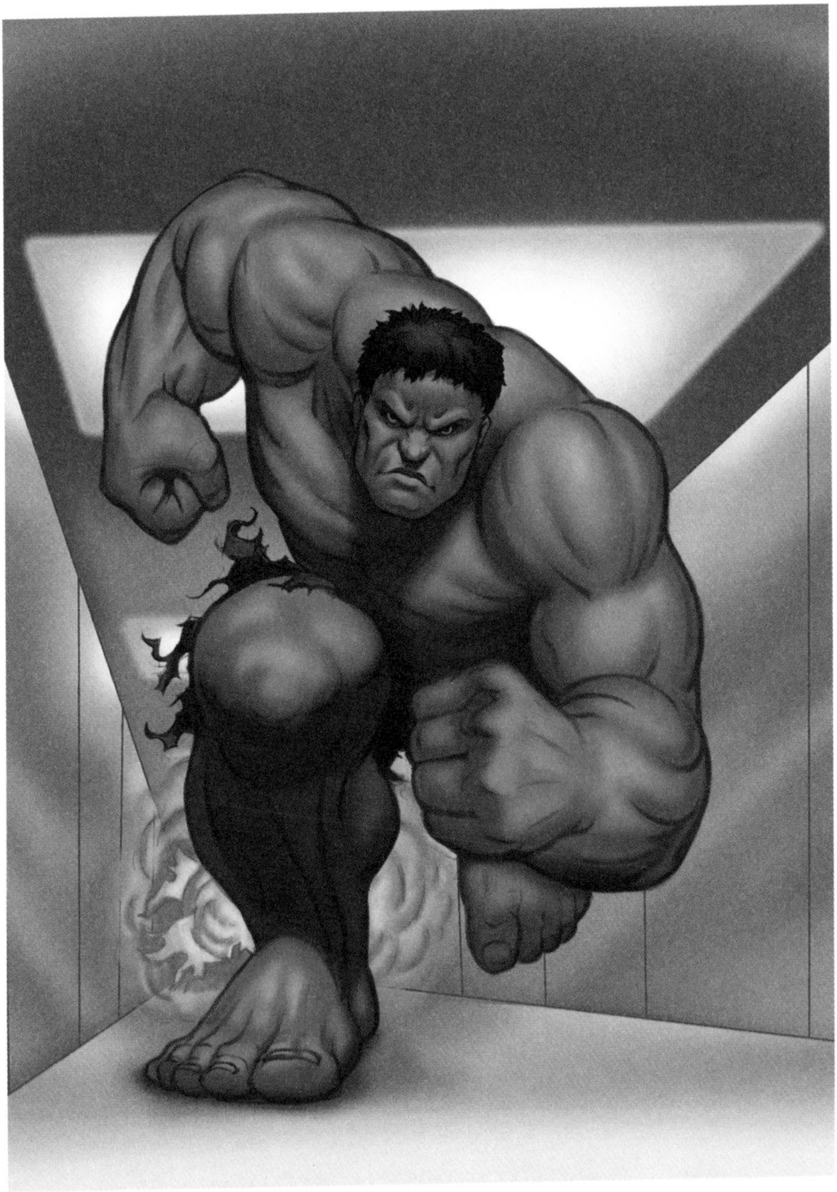

No!

The Hulk is too strong!

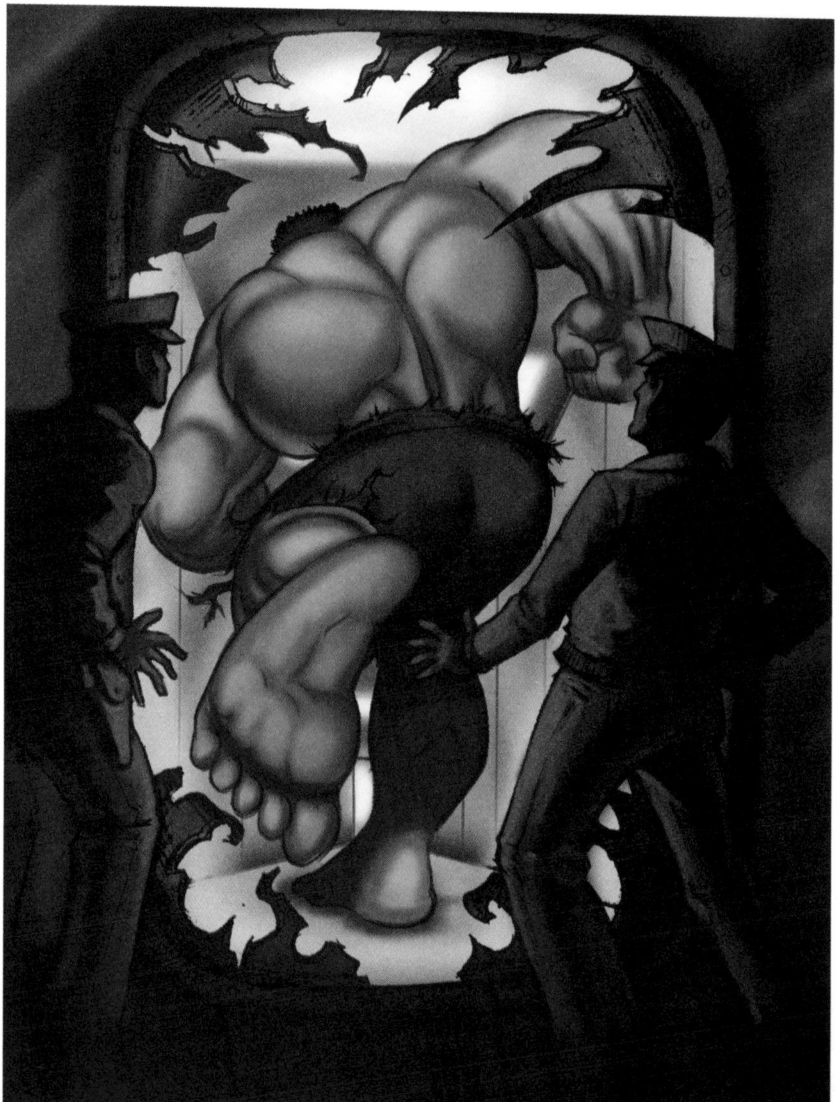

Going, going, gone!

The Hulk escapes.

But not for long.

The Hulk is trapped in a net.

What will he do?

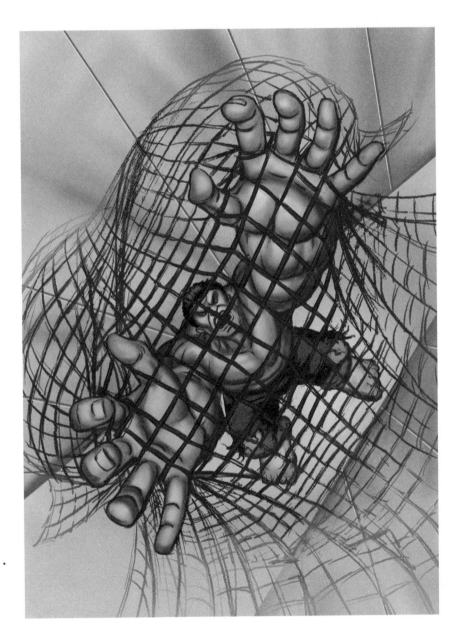

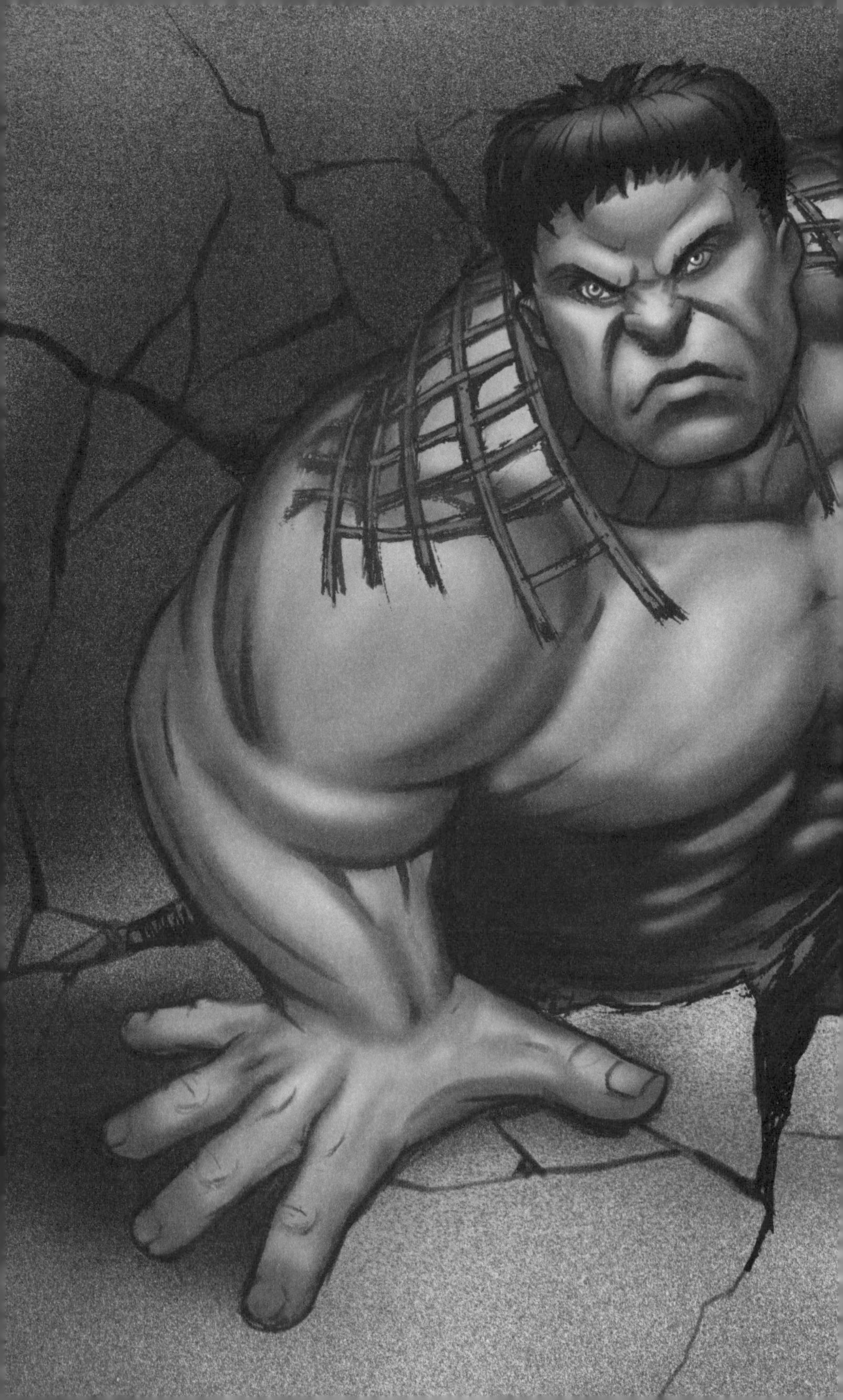

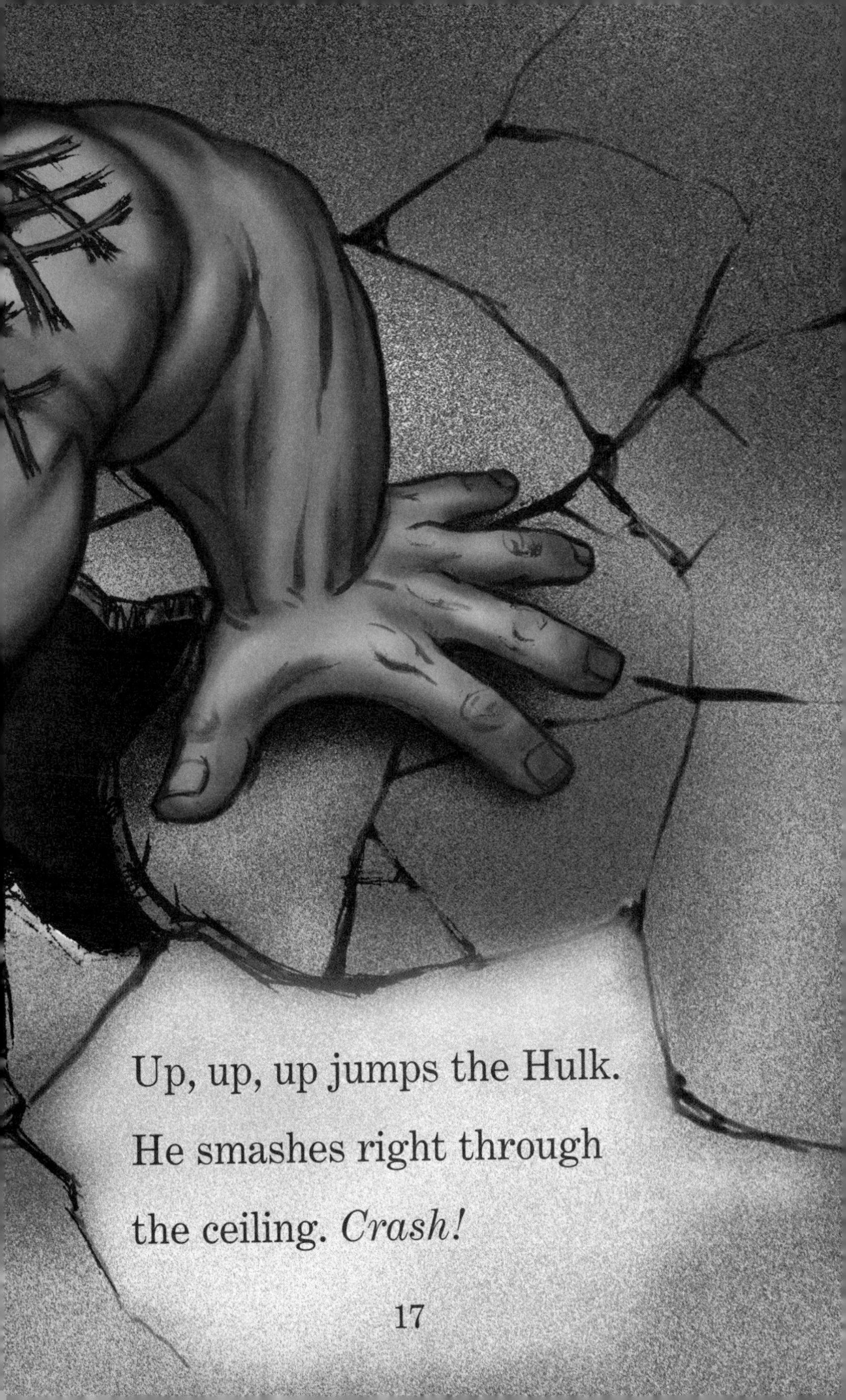

Up, up, up jumps the Hulk.
He smashes right through
the ceiling. *Crash!*

Run, Hulk, run!

The Hulk can outrun anyone.

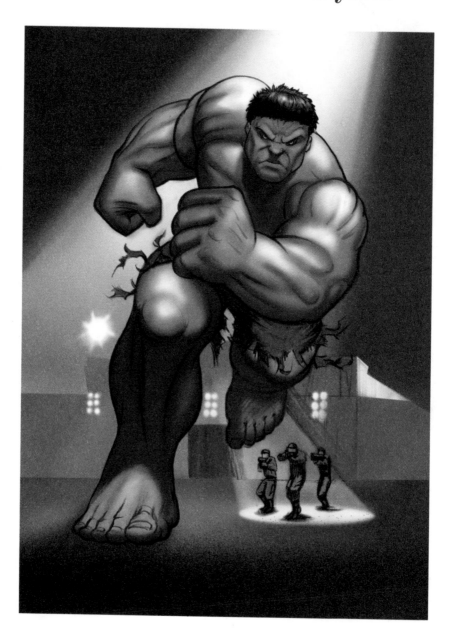

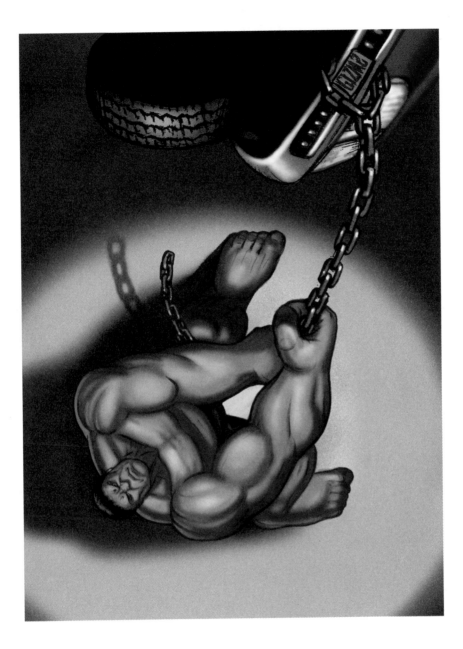

The Hulk can lift anything.

This car is no match for his strength.

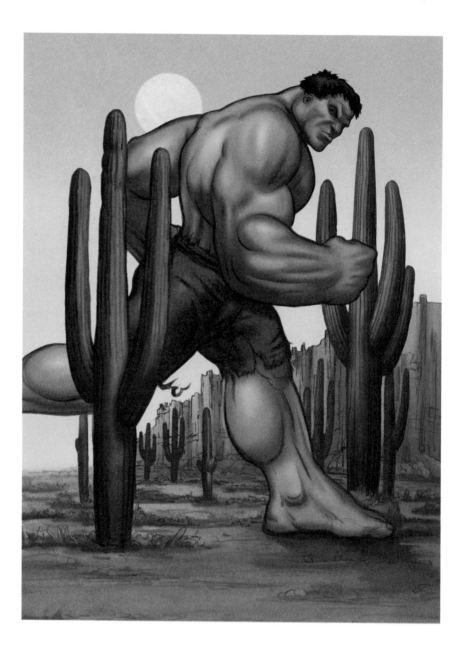

The Hulk has fought off

everything that's come his way.

But he isn't finished yet.

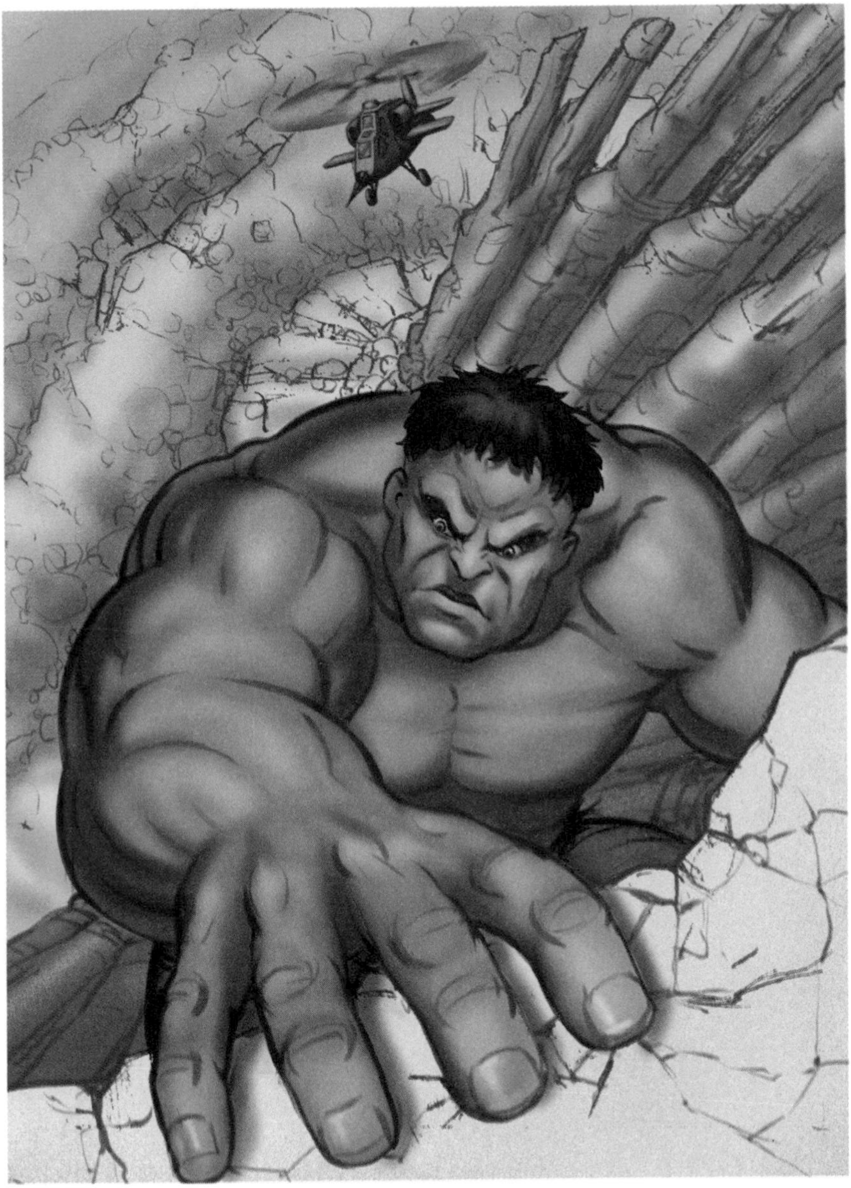

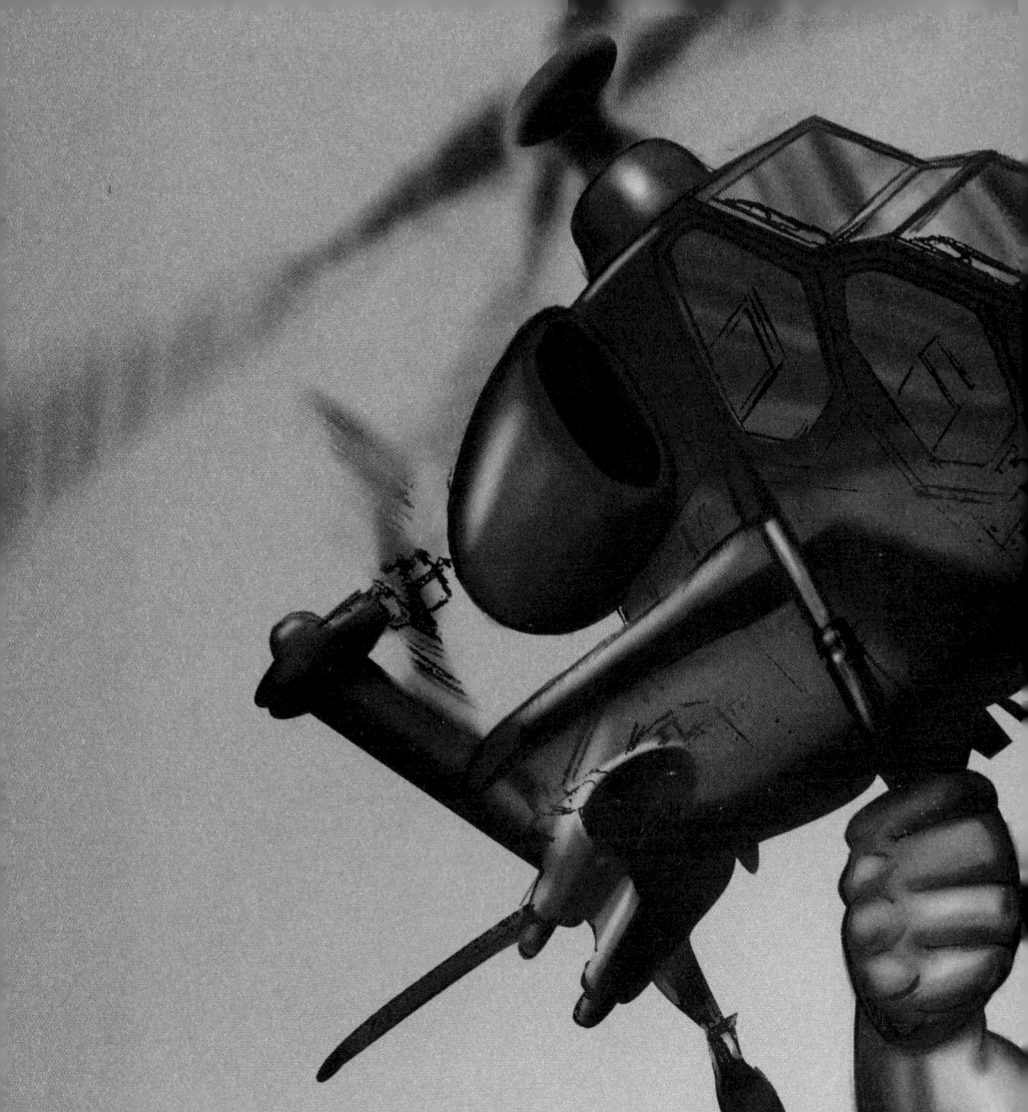

The Hulk takes this helicopter
for a ride deep into the desert.

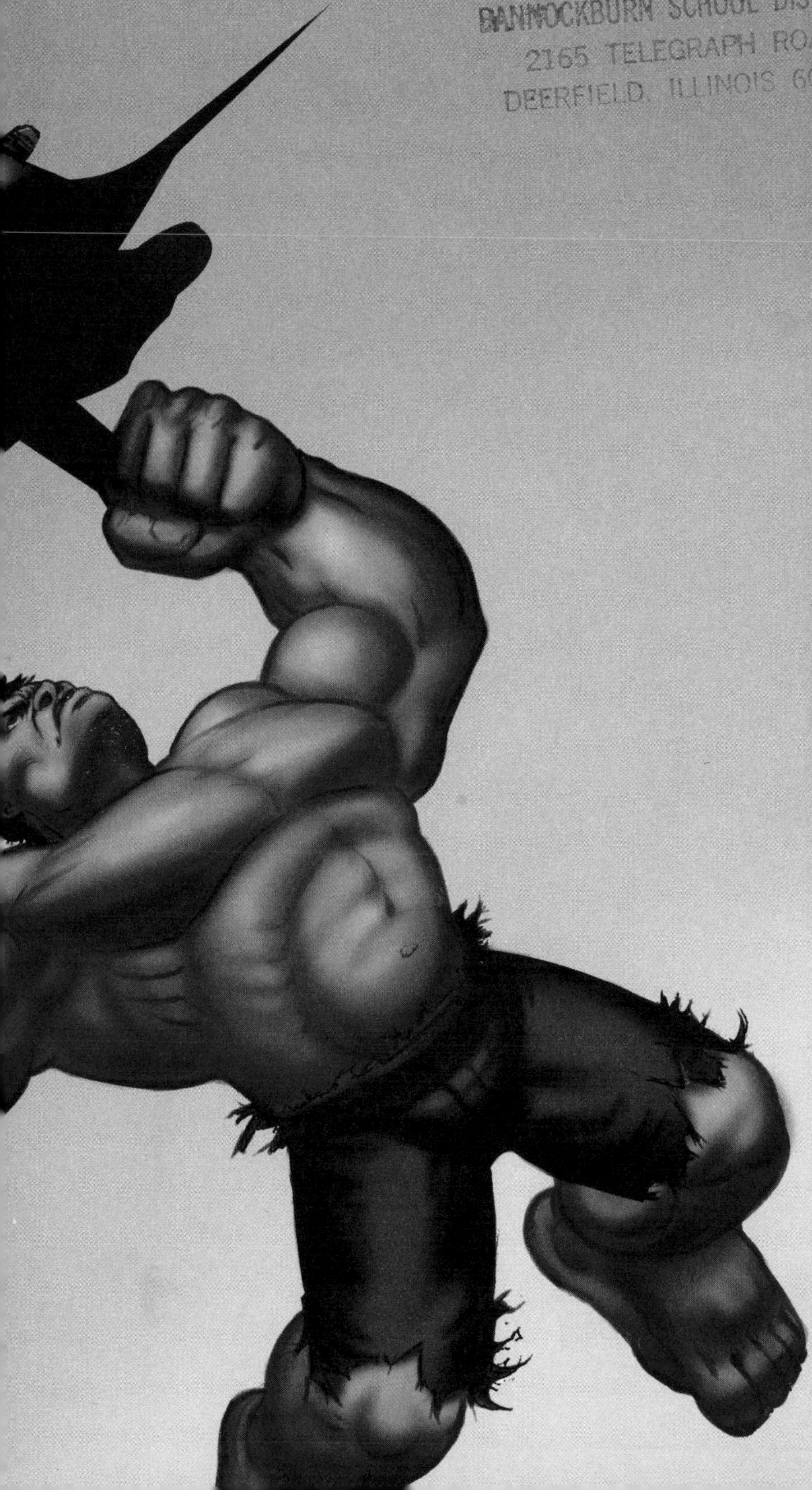

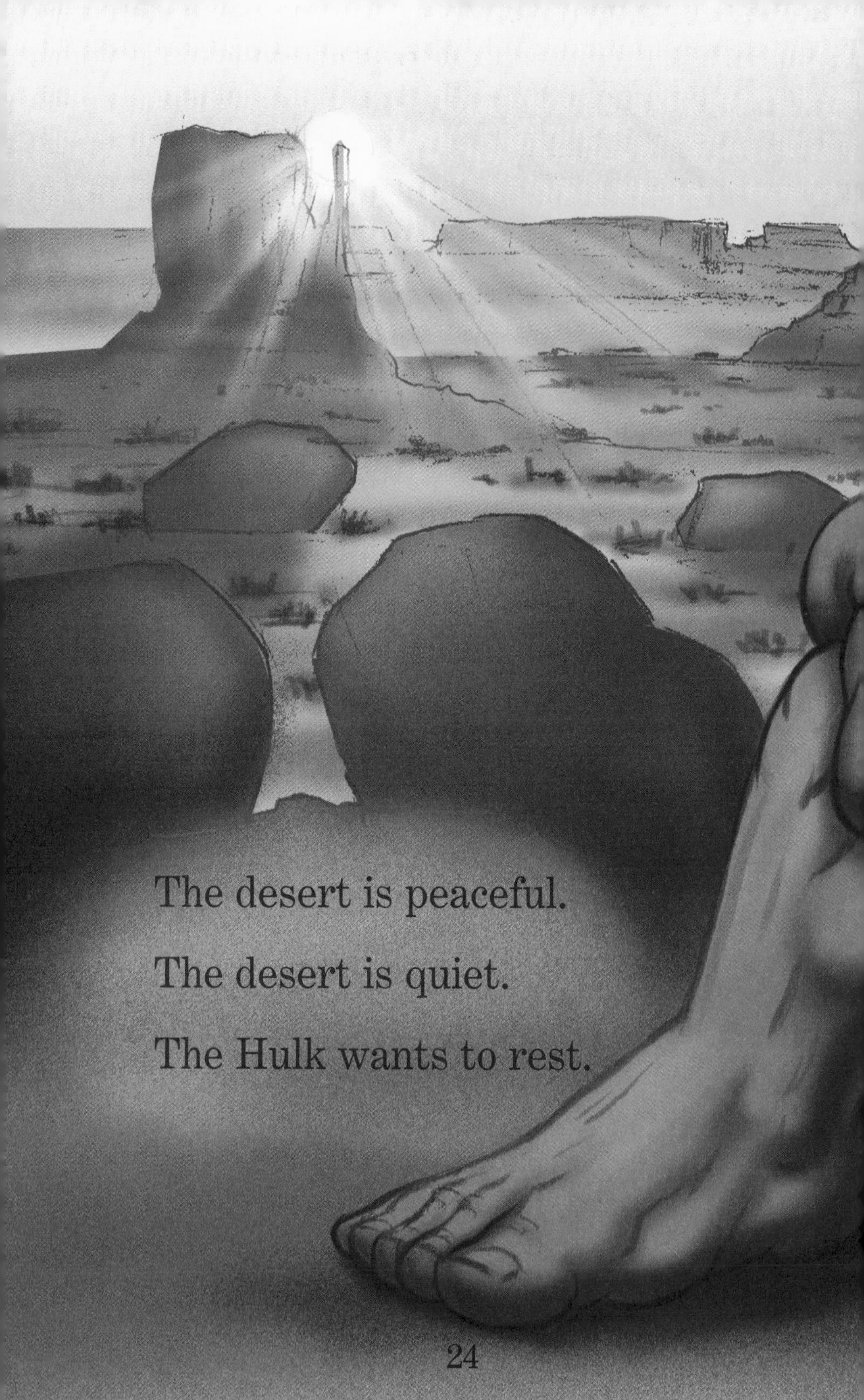

The desert is peaceful.
The desert is quiet.
The Hulk wants to rest.

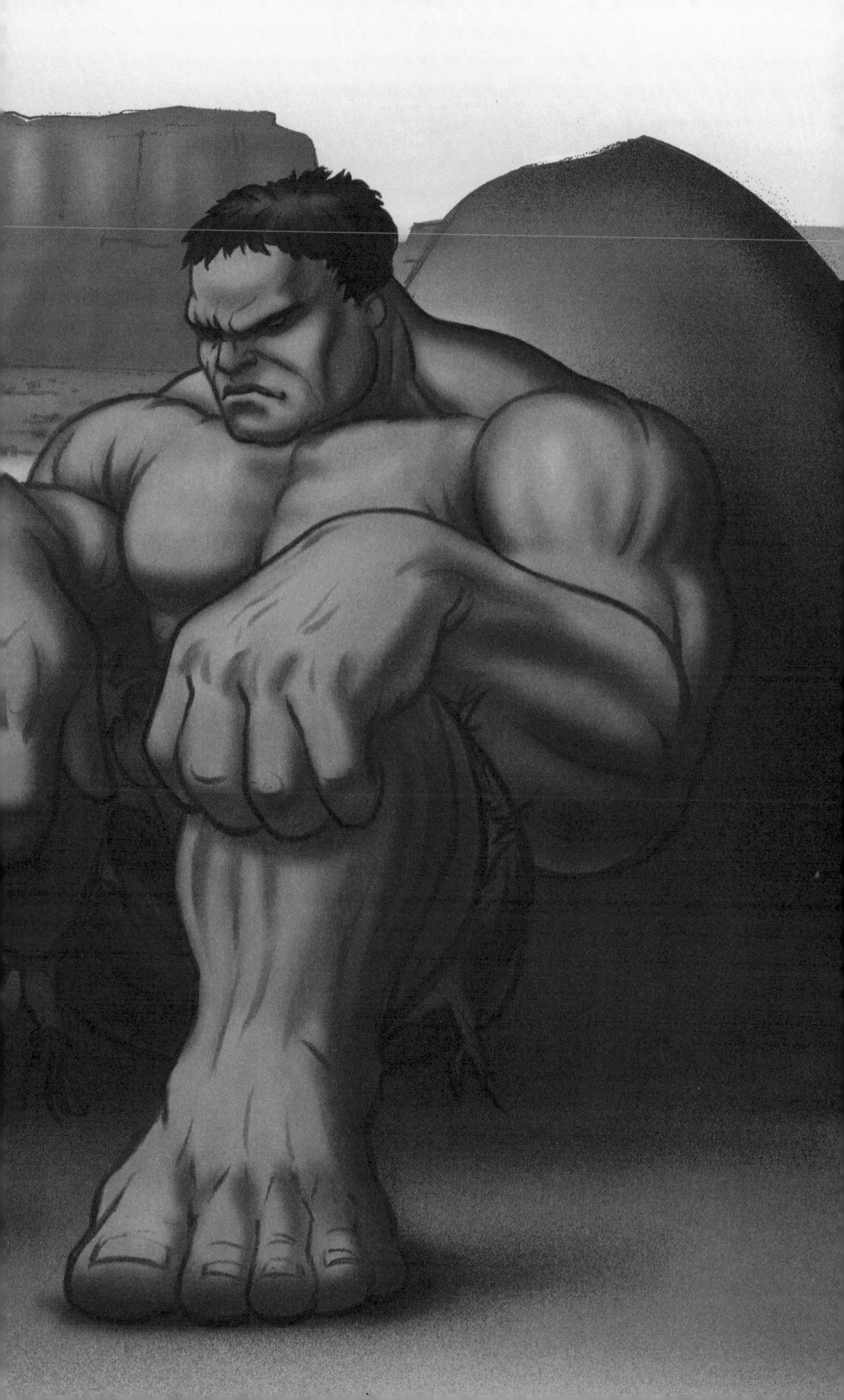

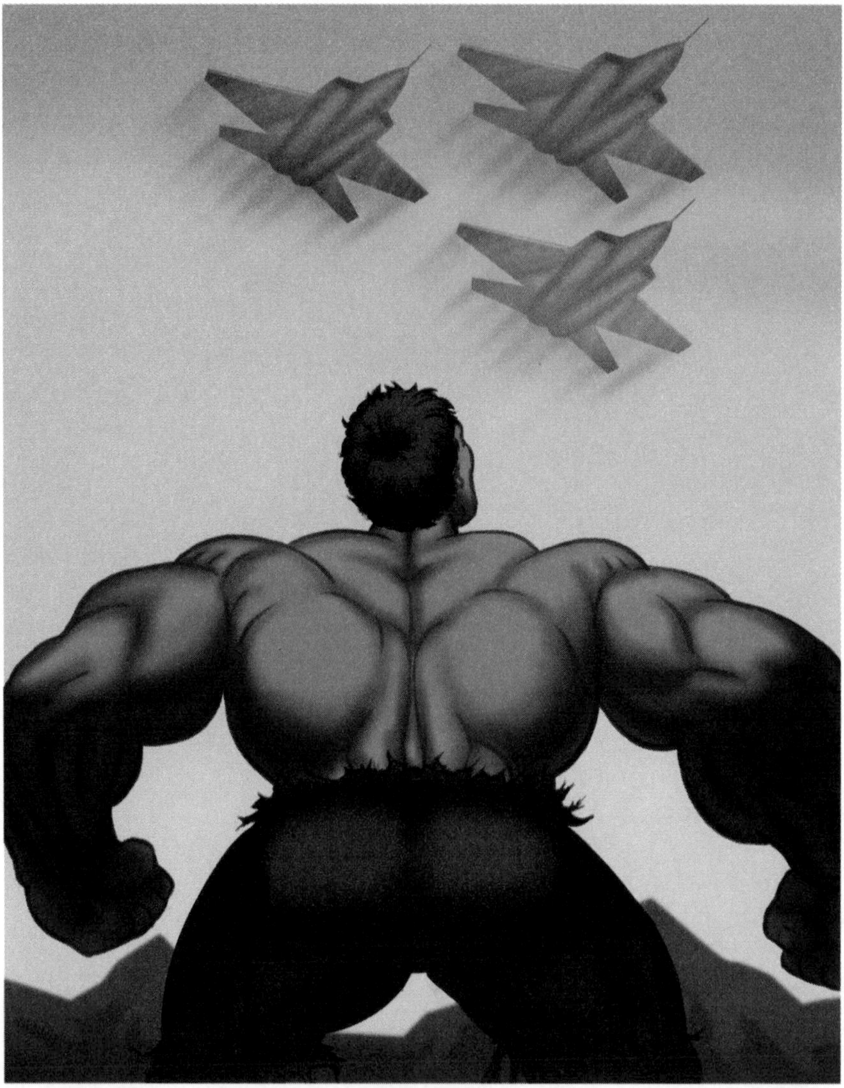

But the scientists won't let the Hulk rest.

Now they have come for him

in jet planes!

The Hulk bounds out of the desert.

The jets fly ahead to cut him off.

The trackers won't give up.

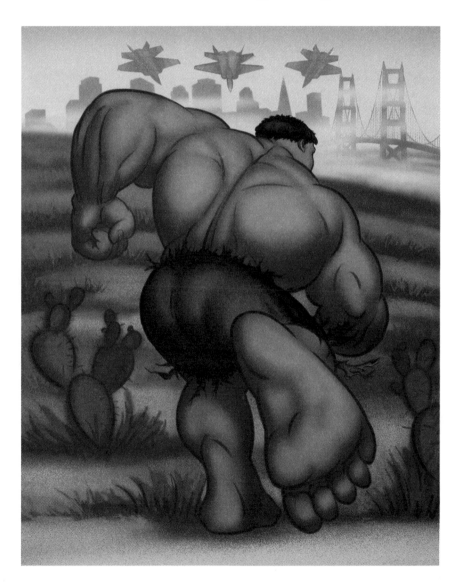

The Hulk is smart.

He knows that there are places jets can't go

The Hulk climbs up the Golden Gate Bridge

as if it were a jungle gym.

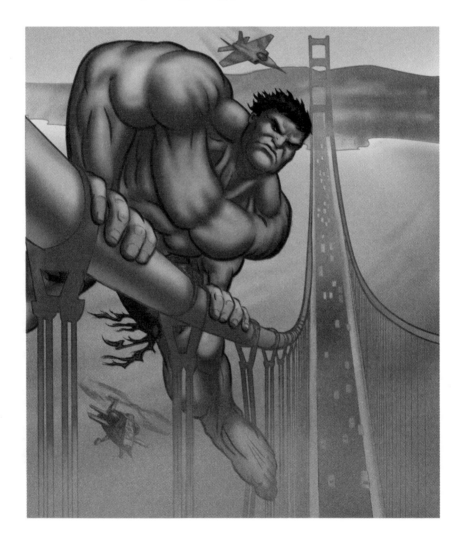

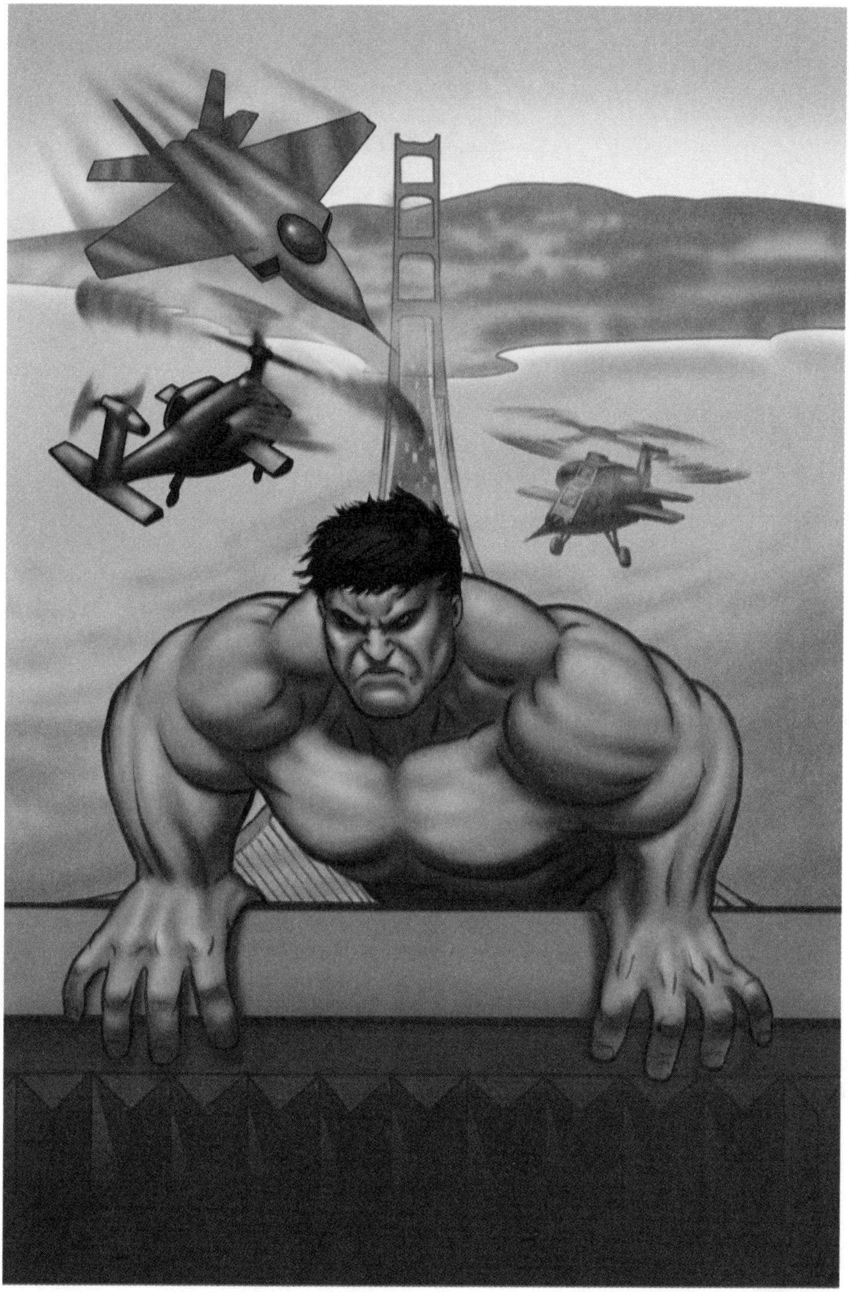

But the scientists keep following.

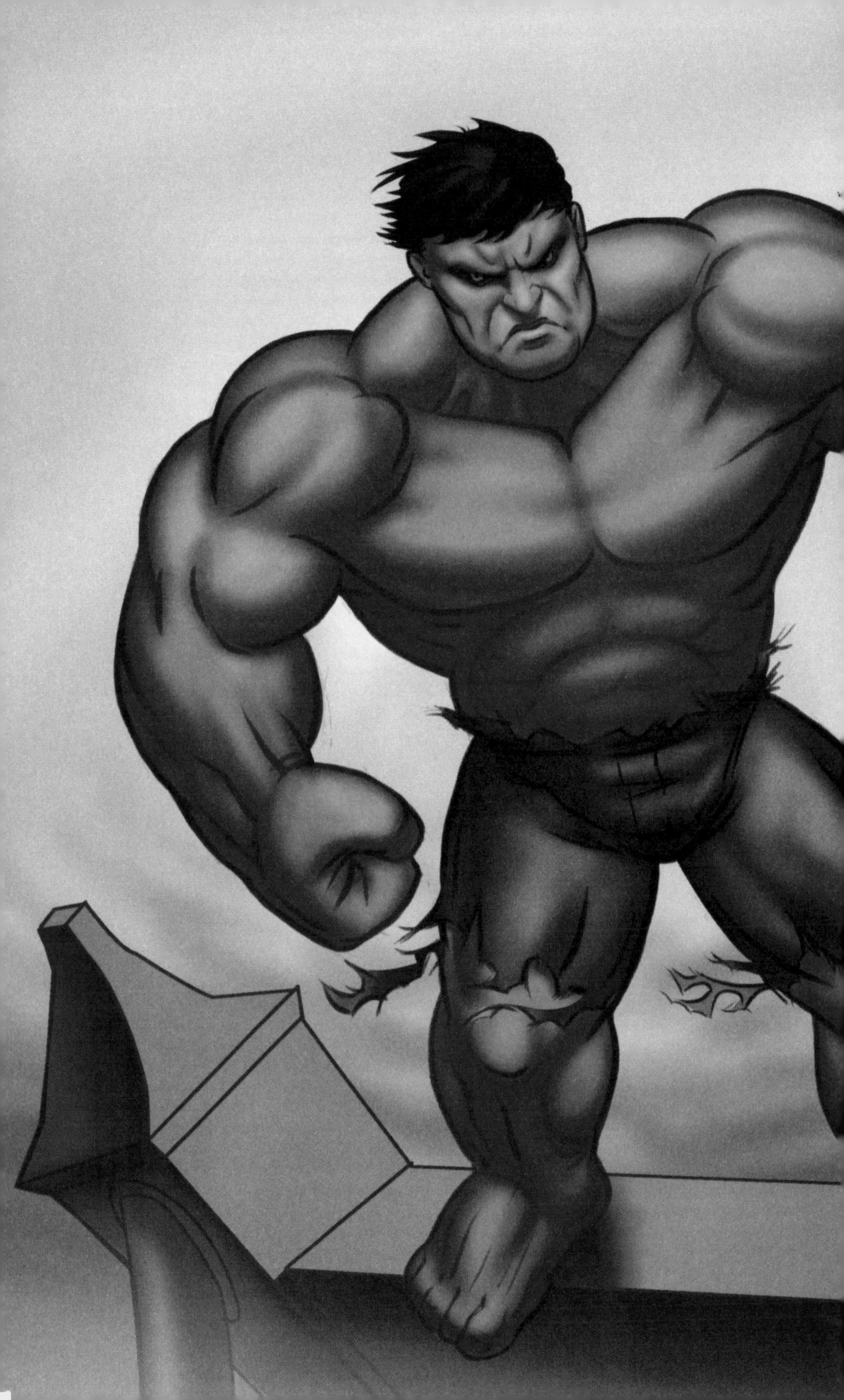

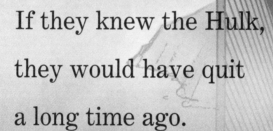

If they knew the Hulk,
they would have quit
a long time ago.

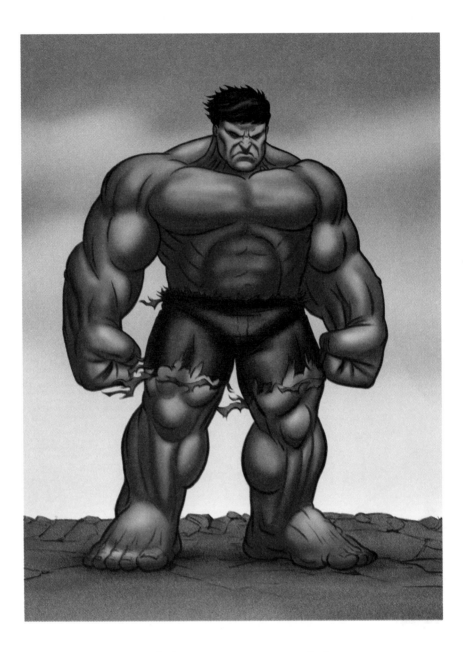

Nothing can stop him.

He's the Hulk.